Copyright © 2002 by Nord-Süd Verlag AG, Gossau Zürich, Switzerland
First published in Switzerland under the title *Annas Islandpony*.
English translation copyright © 2002 by North-South Books Inc., New York

First published in the United States, Great Britain, Canada,
Australia, and New Zealand in 2002 by North-South Books,
an imprint of Nord-Süd Verlag AG, Gossau Zürich, Switzerland.

Distributed in the United States by North-South Books Inc., New York.

Library of Congress Cataloging-in-Publication Data is available.
A CIP catalogue record for this book is available from The British Library.
ISBN 0-7358-1691-3 (trade edition) 10 9 8 7 6 5 4 3 2 1
ISBN 0-7358-1692-1 (library edition) 10 9 8 7 6 5 4 3 2 1
Printed in Belgium

For more information about our books, and the authors and artists
who create them, visit our web site: www.northsouth.com

Winter Pony

By Krista Ruepp

Illustrated by Ulrike Heyne

Translated by J. Alison James

North-South Books
New York/London

It was deep winter in northern Iceland. The horses kept close to the farm in the snow-covered pasture.

Prince, a pony with a silvery mane, lifted his head and cocked his ears as Anna tramped through the snow.

"Prince!" she called. "Prince, come here!"

The little pony trotted over to her. He rubbed his head on her shoulder and nibbled her jacket affectionately.

Anna stroked his mane. Prince was her pony. She had raised him from a foal. He was her best friend.

Winter slowly melted into spring. The snow gave way to spots of brown earth, and day by day it grew warmer.

"Soon we'll take the horses up to the summer pasture," said Anna's father one day.

Anna was shocked. The summer pasture was way up in the mountains! "Not Prince!" she said. "He is too little, Father. He has to stay with me."

"Your pony is nearly a year old. It's time for him to take his place among the herd. If he doesn't go now, he will never fit in," explained her father. "But if you want, you can come along with us."

"I can?" Anna was delighted. Usually only grown-ups went on the long ride into the mountains.

The next day, all the horses were rounded up. Anna rode with her father near the front of the herd. They passed through marshy meadows and saw rocks that steamed from underground hot springs. The mountains looked magical in the morning mist.

But Anna was still worried. Again and again she looked over at Prince. How would he manage without her?

When they reached the summer meadow, the herd was set free. As Prince galloped past Anna, she could barely hold back her tears.

"Take care, Prince," she called sadly.

Anna's father gave her a reassuring hug. "Remember what Grandma always says," he told her. "The mountains are full of mysterious powers. Prince will be safe. Just wait until you see how big he is next winter."

Prince did seem to belong with the herd. When the icy spring storms swept over the mountains, he huddled close together with the other horses.

They stood with their backs to the wind and formed a wall of warmth and protection from the icy rain.

By June the mountains were green and glowing. The herd wandered from one valley to the next, enjoying the warm sun and the sweet grass.

One afternoon when the horses were grazing by a stream, a large chestnut stallion suddenly laid back his ears and snapped at Prince. Frightened, Prince turned and ran away.

The chestnut angrily shook his mane. He galloped after Prince, chasing him to the edge of the cliffs by the waterfall.

Prince was backed into a corner.

The chestnut stamped his forelegs and lunged toward Prince. Both horses reared and bit each other in the neck and legs. With a loud snort, the chestnut gave Prince a strong kick, and Prince fell over the cliff.

Only a narrow mossy ledge saved Prince from falling into the
water far below.

For a long time he lay dazed in the soft moss.

Steam from a hot spring warmed the bed where Prince had
landed, and the crisp mountain air swirled around him. Prince slept
soundly.

Back at the farm, Anna woke up very early that same morning. She had been dreaming about Prince. Something terrible had happened to him. She quickly got dressed and went downstairs. She met her grandmother in the barnyard.

"You're up early, Anna," Grandma cried.

"I couldn't sleep," Anna said. "I had a terrible dream about Prince. I want to go get him and bring him home!"

Grandma took Anna in her arms. "You know, Anna," she said, "life with the herd is as important for your pony as school is for you."

"But what if something happens, and I'm not there to take care of him?"

"Oh, but he's not alone. The horses look out for each other. And if something truly awful happened, the mountain trolls and wood elves would take care of him for you."

"You and your elves, Grandma," Anna said, rolling her eyes. But secretly she felt better.

It is hard to say what helped Prince heal from his fall. Perhaps it was the warm earth, the waterfall's mist, the fresh mountain air. Or maybe it was something more magical. Only the mountains know for sure. But the next morning Prince could stand up. Carefully, he made his way to the top of the cliff.

In the distance Prince saw the herd. He whinnied. Startled, the chestnut lifted his head. Prince went up to him and began to eat from the same tuft of grass. The chestnut kept munching calmly.

The fight was over. Prince had earned the respect of the older horse.

It wasn't long before the nights grew longer and the wind blew cool and crisp.

The farmers went to gather the herd back home, and Anna was allowed to ride along. She was so excited! Where was the herd? Where was Prince?

"Prince!" she called, over and over. "Prince! Prince!"

The horses stormed across the valley in a wild gallop. Prince broke away from the herd and came to Anna. He snorted in her ear and nipped her sweater. Anna laughed out loud. He hadn't forgotten her! He had grown big and strong, just as her father had predicted.

"Thank you," Anna whispered softly, just in case Grandma's elves and trolls were listening.

Prince nuzzled her hand, looking for oats. Anna rubbed his rough mane. "You need a brushing," she said fondly. "But you look wonderful. Come! It's time to go home, my winter pony."